EAT PETE!

Michael Rex

NANCY PAULSEN BOOKS

To my sons, Declan and Gavin,

who make me laugh every day.

NANCY PAULSEN BOOKS
an imprint of Penguin Random House LLC
375 Hudson Street
New York, NY 10014

Library of Congress Cataloging-in-Publication Data
Names: Rex, Michael, author, illustrator.
Title: Eat Pete / Michael Rex.
Description: New York, NY : Nancy Paulsen Books, [2018].
Summary: When a hungry monster appears outside Pete's window, it is not for a
play date, but soon the two are racing toy cars, playing pirate, and more.
Identifiers: LCCN 2017055649 | ISBN 9781524738808 (hardback) | ISBN 9781524738839 (ebook)
Subjects: | CYAC: Monsters—Fiction. | Play—Fiction. | Hunger—Fiction. | Humorous stories.
BISAC: JUVENILE FICTION / Monsters. | JUVENILE FICTION / Humorous Stories.
JUVENILE FICTION / Social Issues / Friendship.
Classification: LCC PZ7.R32875 Eat 2018 | DDC [E]—dc23
LC record available at https://lccn.loc.gov/2017055649

Manufactured in China by RR Donnelley Asia Printing Solutions Ltd.
ISBN 9781524738808
Special Markets ISBN 9781984813909 Not for Resale
10 9 8 7 6 5 4 3 2 1

Design by Dave Kopka.
Text set in Charter ITC Std.
The art was created with pencil, and colored in Photoshop.

This Imagination Library edition is published by Penguin Young Readers, a division of Penguin Random House, exclusively for Dolly Parton's Imagination Library, a not-for-profit program designed to inspire a love of reading and learning, sponsored in part by The Dollywood Foundation. Penguin's trade editions of this work are available wherever books are sold.

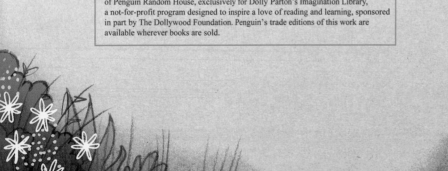

Pete was playing on his bedroom floor when a monster appeared at his window.

"Hi," said Pete. "Do you want to play cars with me?"

The monster didn't want to play cars with Pete. He wanted to . . .

But playing cars looked like fun,
so they had some races.

They set up parking lots.

They made crashes.

"Hey," said Pete, "what should we do next?
Do you want to play pirates?"

The monster did not want to play
pirates with Pete. He wanted to . . .

But the monster had never played pirates before. They dug for treasure.

He walked the plank.

They acted like scallywags!

"Next," said Pete, "I think we should play blocks."

The monster did not want to play blocks with Pete.
He wanted to . . .

But he liked building things,
so they made a castle.

They built towers. They knocked them down.

"Now," said Pete, "we should play superheroes."

The monster did not want to play superheroes with Pete. He wanted to . . .

So he ate him.

The monster piled up some blocks.

He put on the pirate hat.

He spun the wheels of a car.

It wasn't any fun to play alone.

He missed Pete.

So he spat him out.

"That was not very nice!"

Pete told the monster.

"Do you want to play superheroes?" asked Pete.

The monster did not want to play superheroes
with Pete. He wanted to—